The Great Kitty Kidnap

PIP STREET

Jo Simmons

The Great Kitty Kidnap

Illustrated by
Steve Wells

SCHOLASTIC

First published in the UK in 2013 by Scholastic Children's Books
An imprint of Scholastic Ltd
Euston House, 24 Eversholt Street
London, NW1 1DB, UK
Registered office: Westfield Road, Southam, Warwickshire, CV47 0RA
SCHOLASTIC and associated logos are trademarks and/or
registered trademarks of Scholastic Inc.

Text copyright © Joanna Simmons, 2013
Illustrations copyright © Steve Wells, 2013

The right of Joanna Simmons and Steve Wells to be
identified as the author and illustrator of this work
has been asserted by them.

Cover illustration © Steve Wells, 2013

ISBN 978 1 407 14800 7

A CIP catalogue record for this book is available
from the British Library.

Printed and bound by CPI Group (UK) Ltd, Croydon, CR0 4YY
Papers used by Scholastic Children's Books are made from
wood grown in sustainable forests.

1 3 5 7 9 10 8 6 4 2

This is a work of fiction. Names, characters, places, incidents
and dialogues are products of the author's imagination or are used fictitiously.
Any resemblance to actual people, living or dead, events
or locales is entirely coincidental.

www.scholastic.co.uk

www.visitpipstreet.com

For George and Dylan, with all my love.

1

A Street Called Pip

Pip Street looks like an ordinary street, with houses that have doors and windows and roofs, and a bit of front garden at the front and a bit of back garden at the back. It smells like an ordinary street, too – that's to say, of not very much. Except on bin days, when it smells of mushrooms and warm nappies. But – and here's the shocking bit – it doesn't behave like an ordinary street.

No, because strange things are happening on Pip Street. Unexplained events. Mysterious mysteries. Funny stuff! And Bobby Cobbler is about to get caught right in the middle of it.

2

Here's Bobby Cobbler

Bobby Cobbler was a little boy, about this big, with a sprinkling of freckles and teeth as white as snow (and everywhere that Bobby went, his teeth were sure to go). He had sharp eyes (but not sharp enough to cut yourself on), and a mind as curious as a kitten's and fifty times as smart.

Bobby lived on Pip Street. Actually, he was *about* to live on Pip Street. His mum and dad had bought a new home there. Nothing fancy. It wasn't a castle or a palace with golden toilets. It was normal size. Big enough for Bobby, his parents and his cat, Conkers. And for some furniture. And a fridge. And a bath. And some oven gloves. And for Bobby's DVD collection. He had the complete set of *Custard and Chips*, his favourite ever cartoon, and seasons one and two of *Meerkats In Maidstone*, in which a family of meerkats relocates to Maidstone.

Moving house is exciting, isn't it? But Bobby wasn't excited. Nope, he was cross. Grrrr, he was thinking. Bobby had lived in ten different houses and he was only eight years old. Even if you are rubbish at maths, you can tell that's a lot of moving. It's all because Bobby's dad was a travelling sweets salesman. Now that sounds cool, but it's not. For once Bobby's dad had sold his Ninny Drops and Milky Lugs and Sherbet Bumbums to one part of the country, he had to move again, to find new customers. Bobby would be just getting used to one school, just making friends, when *whoops!* it would be moving time again.

5

As the Cobbler car stopped on Pip Street, Bobby reached for the basket next to him. Inside, Conkers, his cat, was feeling cat sick, which is like car sick, only for cats.

"Meow blurrrgghhh," said Conkers.

Conkers was as black as the devil's armpit with shiny eyes, like torches down a well. If he had been a human, he would have been a stuntman or an international footballer who was also amazing at playing the violin. He was just cool. Can pets be cool? Yes, they can. Conkers was proof.

Best of all, Conkers always moved with Bobby. Unlike the friends Bobby had to leave behind, Conkers was portable.

As Bobby and Conkers got out of the car, neither realized that they were being watched. And not just by the pigeon resting in a tree nearby. From a front room on Pip Street, nosy eyes ogled the new arrivals. Who was this mysterious peeper, staring at our new friend and his handsome moggy? And what was he or she muttering quietly? What's that you say, mystery peeper? What is it?

"Nobody does,
nobody does,
nobody does
a whoopsie
on *my* rug!"

3

New Discoveries - Some Good, Some Bad. . .

Bobby spent his first afternoon on Pip Street settling Conkers in. He carried him around the house, tickling him under the chin as he showed him each room. Then the two of them went outside to play and frolic in the garden.

Yes, Conkers was cool, but that doesn't mean he didn't enjoy a little frolic from time to time, and he could always rely on Bobby to join in.

They both jumped in and out of an empty box

nine or ten times.

It was cracking fun!

Then Conkers suddenly got tired and sat on the fence to lick his paws.

In the evening, Bobby unpacked all his books and drawings and paper and rulers and coloured pencils, until his room began to look more like His Room. He collapsed into bed. His mum hadn't found his duvet amongst all the boxes yet, so he slept under some coats. It wasn't so bad. If you put your legs in the arms and your arms in the hoods. . . Bobby fell fast asleep.

The next day it was the next day.

Bobby's mum was busy unpacking when Bobby went downstairs for breakfast. There were boxes everywhere.

"Oh, Bobby," she sighed, "I feel like I'm drowning in boxes."

Can you drown in boxes? wondered Bobby, in his thoughtful way. They weren't very wet, so perhaps not. But his mum didn't look very happy, so he didn't say anything.

Bobby managed to find a packet of crumpets in amongst a box of old Christmas decorations. Then he found the toaster, which was underneath his dad's collection of gravy boats. Finally, he found the fridge, which for some reason was in the downstairs toilet, but luckily had some butter in it. He munched his crumpet sitting on an upturned bucket, then went outside to explore the street.

The houses on Pip Street were mostly at the top, while at the bottom were a few shops and businesses. There was a barber's called

Different Hair
(Because That's What You Come Out With!)

and a cosy-looking cafe called Cafe Coffee, too. At the very end there was a newsagent called This Is The News! It had a few handwritten adverts in its window. Bobby read them. There was an advert for a new pancake place that had just opened, called **Pete's Pancake Pit Stop**, and two cards, each giving details of missing cats.

That's when Bobby remembered. With a wobbly feeling in his stomach, like you get when you read comics in the car, he realized he hadn't seen Conkers since yesterday afternoon. This wasn't right. Conkers usually came to bed with Bobby, to give him a good nose-butting before settling down. Conkers was used to moving house, too, he had done it so often. He knew not to run off. Not only was he cool, he was sensible, too.

Bobby ran home and began searching for his cat. He turned over boxes and hunted behind furniture and ran all over the garden calling "Conkers, Conkers" until he nearly went bonkers.

Nothing.

He needed to look further away, he thought, running out on to the street again and colliding with a tiny pixie dressed as a pirate being chased by an enormous bear.

"Oh my sprinkles!"

shouted Bobby.

"What was that?"

As it turns out it wasn't a pixie and a bear at all, it was Imelda and her brother Nathan.

"Who are you?" asked Imelda, pointing her cutlass at Bobby, her red curly hair blazing in the sun.

"I'm Bobby. I live here at number four. Who are you?" said Bobby.

"Your neighbour!" shouted Imelda, waving her cutlass above her head. "I live right next door. I'm Imelda – Imelda Alice Marjorie Small!" (Which, if you write it out, makes

I AM Small – and she was.) Imelda only came up to Bobby's elbows, but she was no baby. She was smart and tough and full of energy, with a look in her eyes as fierce as lemons.

Imelda flung down her weapon and skipped over to shake Bobby's hand.

"This is my older brother, Nathan. Nathan Octavius Troy Small." (Which, if you write it out, makes NOT Small – and he wasn't.)

Nathan, who was dressed in a brown dressing gown, ambled over and shook Bobby's hand.

Nathan seemed the opposite of his sister. She was tiny and fizzy, like a chemistry experiment by a mad scientist, but he was tall and slow with a relaxed face, like a sleepy puppy that's just remembered a lovely meal it once had.

Bobby explained he was looking for his cat.

"I've never seen your cat, but I'll help you find him," said Imelda, waving her cutlass again. For Imelda loved a mystery and a challenge and besides, it was three days into the summer holidays and she was bored already.

"Can I come to your house?" asked Imelda, racing towards Bobby's front door.

Imelda had a forceful personality. It was hard to say no to her. So Bobby said yes, and showed her in, as Nathan ambled back home.

"Mum, this is Imelda from next door," said Bobby, introducing the pint-sized pirate.

"Pleased to meet you," said Bobby's mum, from behind a huge box that contained sixteen saucepans, a camping stove, three torches, a bicycle pump and a set of steak knives in a presentation case.

The children went upstairs to pace and think and think and pace.

"Let's search the neighbourhood," said

Imelda, swiping her cutlass. "Let's open all the garages! Let's dig up all the gardens! Let's hunt in the bushes to find Conkers. We must find him. To the rescue, come on! CHARGE!"

"Or we could put up some posters?" said Bobby, as Imelda was about to sprint out of the door.

"Posters!" shouted Imelda. "Yes! I like it! Double dangerous doughnuts, Bobby!

Posters are it!"

4

Missing!

So Bobby and Imelda got to work. They wrote

MISSING

CONKERS
THE CAT

out poster after poster after poster, until they had a lot of posters. On each one they wrote **MISSING** – CONKERS THE CAT. LOOKS LIKE A MINIATURE

BLACK PANTHER (ON A GOOD DAY). PLEASE
RETURN TO BOBBY AT NUMBER 4 PIP STREET.

Imelda went home to get some sticky tape, and
her brother Nathan too. Then the three of them
raced all over the neighbourhood, splattering
it with the **MISSING** posters like they were
wallpapering the world.

They soon discovered that there were **MISSING** posters everywhere. Someone had lost their favourite cardigan, somewhere on Pip Street. A three year old had lost his lunch box, with the lunch still inside (a double blow). There was even a poster with a photo of a pen on it, saying HAVE YOU SEEN MY BLUE PEN?

But worse than mislaid woollies and absent pens were the missing cats! On every tree and lamp post, posters showed sad cat faces peering out with MISSING underneath. Tibbles and Kibbles and Felix and Shmelix and Pockets and Patches and Brian and Leslie and Bartholomew Garlic Bread Kittenpuss the Third – all missing.

"Where are all these cats going?" said Bobby, frowning. "It's not normal for so many cats to go missing at once."

"Did they all go on holiday to Scotland, do you think?" said Imelda.

But that would have been impossible, thought

Bobby. Everybody knows cats hate Scotland in the summer. They can't stand the midges.

With just one poster left, the three returned to Pip Street.

"Let's stick one on that tree by Mother Pie's house," suggested Nathan.

Mother Pie was a blue-haired old lady with all the usual old lady trimmings: sensible flat shoes, sensible beige coat, sensible tartan shopping trolley which she did NOT fill with tiny dogs wearing bows in their fur.

That would have been very unsensible and that wasn't Mother Pie's way. Everyone on Pip Street thought she was just a bog-standard harmless old dropsicle. But one thing stood out about Mother Pie – she had a terrible blinking habit. Not normal flickery blinks, but great big face-scrunching blinks. When Mother Pie blinked, it was like her whole face jumped; like something inside was trying to escape and she was fighting to keep it in.

"Who is Mother Pie?" asked Bobby.

"Just an old wrinkly who is really very blinky," said Imelda.

"Is she stinky, too?" asked Bobby.

"Not really," said Imelda, looking disappointed.

26

"She smells of marshmallows."

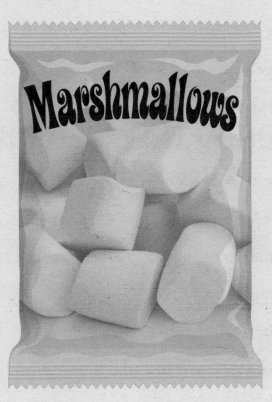

5

Bobby Thinks About the Kitty Nitty Gritty

All afternoon Bobby thought about Conkers and the other missing cats. Bobby was good at thinking. He was what you might call "thoughtful".

His mother took him to Different Hair (he came out with a lopsided fringe and a curl over one ear). He thought about the cats.

His mother took him to the supermarket to buy

beefy crinkles and parsnip fritters and caramel for dinner. He thought about the cats.

When Bobby got home, he climbed into a sleeping bag and rolled around on the floor pretending to be a giant maggot. And still thought about the cats.

When Bobby took his bike out and almost rode into a gigantic dog poo, sitting on the pavement like an overweight toad, well, at that point Bobby did not think about the cats. He thought about doing an emergency swerve.

CLEAN THIS UP –
DOGGIE DOINGS WILL
BE OUR RUINS!!!!!!!!

And then did an emergency swerve.

Luckily, someone had drawn a large circle around the poo in chalk saying **CLEAN THIS UP – DOGGIE DOINGS WILL BE OUR RUINS** with about fifteen exclamation marks, which I can't be bothered to type out here.

Bobby silently thanked whoever had chalked that warning and saved him from a terrible accident. Who was the ultra-hygienic, community-minded person (who also had a nice flair for rhymes) behind the pavement message?

6

Introducing Jeff the Chalk

It was Jeff the Chalk, that's who! But of course you haven't met him yet. So sorry, my mistake.

Jeff the Chalk lived next door to Mother Pie at number 1, Pip Street. He was tall and skinny, with fine, dark hair.

No one knew much about him, except that he wrote messages in chalk. Mostly, he wrote on pavements, about dog poos. Not just about them, but around them. Nobody was sure when he went out to write his anti-doggy-plop messages. Perhaps the middle of the night? Jeff was a bit of a mystery.

One thing was certain as Tuesdays: he was on a one-man mission to make dog owners clear up after their dogs. Because you know what the trouble with dog mess is? It's

really,

really

messy.

7

Clues From the Cat Map

After his near-poo experience, Bobby decided to stop riding his bike and went upstairs to draw a map. The map, which he called a Cat Map (or *kitty carte* in French), showed where all the cats had gone missing from. A pattern emerged. They had all lived on Pip Street and the next two streets along, Chip Street and Dip Street.

"Hmmm," said Bobby, in his thoughtful way.

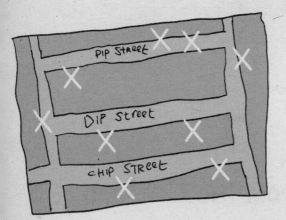

What was nearby that might tempt a cat away? A fish-finger factory? A giant outdoor radiator with fur beds attached? Bobby wasn't sure. He was only just getting to know Pip Street and the streets nearby. He needed Imelda and Nathan's help again, and rushed round to talk to them.

Imelda came to the door wearing a Tudor lord costume.

"Good morrow to you, sir!" she cried as she

34

opened the door. "What bringeth thee hither this fine day?"

Bobby showed Imelda and Nathan the map.

"It doesn't make sense," said Nathan. "There's nothing to tempt a cat away around here. Just normal, quiet streets. Oh, and over there is Rabid Pug Wood, but that's not somewhere anyone, human or cat, wants to visit."

"I' faith, sir, 'tis a fearful place," said Imelda, shuddering in a Tudor way (if that's possible). "No, but really, Bobby, it's super scary," she added.

"Legend has it that a tiny dog with a creasy nose and a slobbering disease walks those woods," said Nathan, pulling his brown dressing

35

gown around him. "On

a still night,

you can

hear him

snuffling

in the

bushes,

licking up

baby woodlice

from rotten logs for

his tea. They say one bite is all it takes. You are

bitten. And then, dead."

Bobby shivered.

"Anyway, let's have another look outside," said Nathan, guessing how worried Bobby was about Conkers. "We've still got an hour before dinner."

"God's bodkins, sires," said Imelda. "Let us make for the street betimes and find that missing cat right now!"

They searched under cars. Nothing. They peeped through hedges. Nothing. They squinted up drainpipes. Nothing. They peered into drains.  Nothing. They scanned the trees. Nothing. (Well, that pigeon was still there – perhaps his feet were glued to the branch? Or maybe he was just lazy. . . What do you mean, what pigeon?

The one from page seven, of course! Come on, keep up!)

Tired, disappointed and hungry, the children went home, completely and utterly cat-less.

Bobby's mum was busy grilling the beefy crinkles for dinner when he got in. He told her about the disappearances.

"Cats go missing all the time, Bobby," she said. "I'm sure if any cat can find his way home, Conkers can."

"But I think someone is taking them," said Bobby. "It can't just be a coincidence."

"Taking what?" said Bobby's dad, marching in and dumping fifteen boxes of Tupenny Twit Bits on the kitchen table.

"All the cats from the neighbourhood," said Bobby.

"Oh fa-la-la, Bobby," said his Dad, opening the boxes busily. "Who is going to steal cats? Pip Street is just a normal, quiet street, not some sort of horrible home for hard-nut, crime-mad criminals! Now mind out," he added. "I've got forty bags of Sparkling Jims and a sack of Lady Brittles to bring in."

Dad never listens to me, thought Bobby, as his dad rushed out. But he didn't say it, because as well as being a thoughtful boy, he had nice manners. He was what you might call "polite".

That night, Bobby couldn't sleep. Usually, he liked the night. It was quieter than the day.

Not as many cars. Fewer buses. Practically no penny-farthings. He liked to peep out at the night and look at the moon and think mellow night-time thoughts that sometimes went on for twenty minutes or more.

But as Bobby peeped at the moon this very night, he felt sadder than an old granddad who has lost his favourite hankie. His brain was like a washing machine, with questions whirling round like pants on a spin cycle. Would he ever see Conkers again? Or stroke his ears? Or accidentally step on his tail? He had looked everywhere and now his only hope was the posters. But with so many cats missing, what chance was there of Conkers being found? Or that blue pen?

A giant tear roller-skated down Bobby's freckly cheek, and splashed into salty sparkles on his chest. Another followed. Bobby rubbed it away. Yet another was brewing when suddenly, a movement caught Bobby's eye and stopped his crying.

A door was opening.
The door to Mother
Pie's house. And out
she came, with her

beige coat on, pulling
her tartan shopping
trolley behind her.

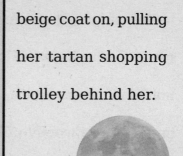

She must be going to the shops for some suckie sweets or whatever old ladies like, thought Bobby. But shouldn't old ladies be sitting by a fire, knitting woolly pullies at this time of night? Where was she going? And wait a second . . . why did she have a padlock on her shopping trolley?

8

Suspects!

After a night of sleeping in his bed wearing pyjamas, Bobby woke up. It was the morning, sure as morning follows night.

"Cockadoodledo," said a cockerel, on a farm somewhere.

Unfortunately, there was still no sign of Conkers. When Bobby went downstairs for breakfast, he thought he saw Conkers, from the

corner of his eye, curled

up in the armchair with

the sun warming his black

fur. It made his heart leap,

then crash back down with

disappointment when he

realized it was just a black jumper.

To cheer himself up, Bobby thought about his

birthday in ten days' time. His Great Auntie Mo,

who lived in Glen Haggis in faraway Scotland,

always sent him a gift. Great Auntie Mo was a

great auntie – literally. She brought Bobby special

Scottish toffees when she came to visit and taught

him ancient Scottish words like "hootenanny",

"shortbread" and "the noo".

Great Auntie Mo was a bit of a dreamer. She had a big imagination and a big heart. She often sent Bobby super-bonkers presents, but he loved her for that. Forget boring book tokens, one year Great Auntie Mo sent him an envelope of leprechaun sighs. Another time, she sent him some snow leopard fur. Bobby knew it was just fluff from the back of the sofa. But it's the thought that counts, he thought. And as we know, Bobby was *very* thoughtful.

He gave Great Auntie Mo a call to tell her about Conkers going missing. It was always good to talk to Great Auntie Mo.

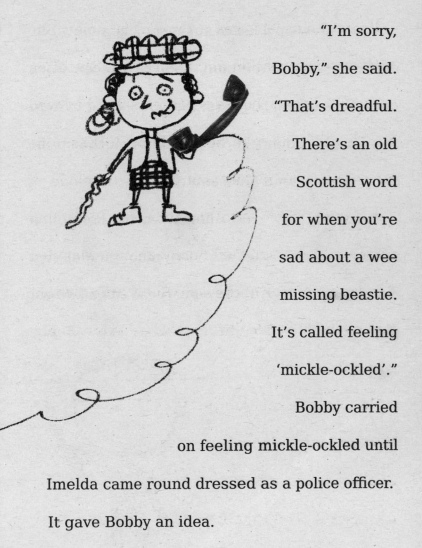

"I'm sorry, Bobby," she said. "That's dreadful. There's an old Scottish word for when you're sad about a wee missing beastie. It's called feeling 'mickle-ockled'."

Bobby carried on feeling mickle-ockled until Imelda came round dressed as a police officer. It gave Bobby an idea.

"Let's draw up a list of suspects, like they do on detective shows," he said. "Maybe we can work out who is taking the cats. But you'll have to help me, Imelda. I don't know who lives on the street yet. I've only been here two days."

"I *can* do that!" said Imelda, waving her police officer's hat in the air "Dripping dingleberry doughnuts, Bobby! I know everyone. When do we get started?"

9

The List

When you've got something to start, you might as well get started on starting it straight away. That's what Bobby and Imelda thought, and so they started drawing up a list of Pip Street people. The list, which they code-named T H E L I S T,

looked like this

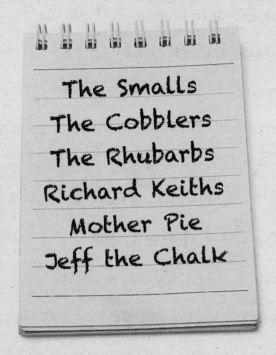

The Smalls
The Cobblers
The Rhubarbs
Richard Keiths
Mother Pie
Jeff the Chalk

The Rhubarb family lived next door to Bobby at number 6. There were twin girls, Cinnamon and Bathsheba, who were fifteen and mad about theatre and plays. They wanted to act, like their mum, Felicity. She played an antiques shop owner in the soap opera *Gubbings*. Their dad, Crispin, was an actor, too. He had appeared in all the best plays, including *She Wore Pancakes in Her Hair*, *Lady Cristobel's Toaster* and the hilarious comedy *Time and Time and Time and Time Again*.

"Next to them is Richard Keiths," said Imelda. "He goes everywhere on a mobility scooter. Can you take a cat on a mobility scooter?"

"Unlikely," said Bobby, "but we need to question him."

"Then there's Mother Pie," said Imelda.

"She looks harmless," said Bobby. "But she does like to stay up late. I saw her going out to the shops with her trolley last night."

"Finally, there's Jeff the Chalk," said Imelda.

"He's very private. Nobody knows much about him, but I think he's just shy. He always smiles when he sees me, anyway."

"I'd say he's a suspect," said Bobby. "The only thing we know about him is that he hates pet mess. Maybe he got tired of chalking and started chasing instead?"

10

A Right Royal Snoop Around

It's all fine and smashing having a list of suspects, but could Bobby and Imelda just march up to everyone and ask them if they'd been up to any feline funny business? Of course they could not. So what should they do? Just as they were thinking this over, some good fortune landed on their heads, like the luckiest seagull poo ever.

Bobby's mum was collecting money for the

charity St Ticklebiscuits,

which takes cats and dogs

from poor homes on holidays.

"Why don't you and Imelda

go collecting on the street?"

Bobby's mum suggested. "It will

give you something to do. I've

already popped a few coins in

and so has Dad, to get you started. . ."

The children jumped at the chance,

understanding at exactly the same second that

this was the perfect excuse for a right royal snoop

around.

"This is the perfect excuse for a right royal

snoop around," said Bobby.

"That's *just* what I was thinking!" said Imelda.

They knocked at the Rhubarbs' house first.

"How marvellous, children," said Mrs Rhubarb,

smiling. "Cats and dogs deserve a holiday just as

much as we do! Such special

little creatures, aren't they?

I can't tell you

how much I

miss our cat,

Coriolanus,

since he

disappeared."

Mrs Rhubarb

sighed, sadly.

"Disappeared?" asked Bobby.

"Yes. He hasn't been seen in five days. I cannot imagine where he's got to. Such a delicate soul. He's not used to life outdoors. . ." And she plopped some coins into the collecting tin.

The children gave Mrs Rhubarb a St Ticklebiscuits badge, then Bobby wrote on THE LIST: NOT GUILTY – CAT MISSING, TOO!!

Next they knocked on Richard Keiths' door, but he was out.

"Probably at the Co-op buying crisps," said Imelda. "Richard Keiths loves crisps, the saltier the better."

They moved on to Mother Pie's house.

"Hello, Imelda," Mother Pie said as she shuffled

on to the doorstep in her beige slippers. "And who

do we have here?"

Before Imelda could answer, Mother Pie

blinked, her face

squidging into a

million creases,

looking like one

of those forgotten,

crumpled pairs of pants

discovered at the very

bottom of the pant drawer.

"This is Bobby," said Imelda. "He's just

moved here so he's new and doesn't know anything about Pip Street, but we're going to be friends and solve mysteries and do adventures."

"Shhh," said Bobby, elbowing her in the ribs.

"And what mysteries might these be?" asked Mother Pie, blinking so hard that her face looked as though it were pogo-ing.

"Nothing, really, except that I've lost my cat," said Bobby, looking down shyly.

"Well, I'm sure I don't know anything about cats going missing, I'm sure I don't," said Mother Pie. "What can I do for you?"

"Collecting for St Ticklebiscuits, please!" said Imelda, thrusting the tin into Mother Pie's face.

The old lady flinched like she'd smelt the terrible smell of mouldy custard mixed with joggers' socks.

"Come in and put one of those charming badges on my coat, will you, children, while I find some change," she said.

Mother Pie's coat was hanging in the hall. Imelda put the tin down on a table next to a photo of Mother Pie when she was young, standing on a beautiful rug.

The children stuck the badge to her coat and heard the *chink chink* of the collecting tin as Mother Pie dropped in her contribution.

As they left, Bobby wrote next to her name: DENIES CAT STEALING.

"Only Jeff the Chalk left now," said Imelda.

They walked up to Jeff's house. The front garden was very neat. Nothing stirred, not even a mouse, which, given that all the cats in the neighbourhood had disappeared, was surprising. You'd think the mice would be making the most of it.

Bobby knocked.

Smash! went something inside. A plate? Being dropped? Then silence. Then a curtain in the living room twitched. More silence.

"Are we being watched?" whispered Imelda.

"I don't know," whispered Bobby, "but let's not stick around to find out."

And they raced back to Bobby's house.

Inside, Bobby's mum opened the tin.

"Let's see how you got on," she smiled, tipping the contents on to the kitchen table.

Out tumbled four pound coins, some 2p pieces, three brown buttons, six carrot slices and a badge that said I ♡ **Marshmallows**.

"Who would put all that mucky old rubbish in the tin?" said Bobby, with a thoughtful look on his face (and some string and an old tissue in his pocket).

Who indeed?

11

Richard Keiths Points His Finger of Blame

Feeling puzzled and muddled, Bobby and Imelda wandered back on to Pip Street.

"What does all this mean?" said Imelda, "and *why* does all this mean? And when? And can I have a biscuit? I'm starving."

But there was no time for answers or biscuits, not even little ones like Iced Gems, because at that minute Richard Keiths came hurtling up the pavement on his mobility scooter.

Richard Keiths lived at number 8 Pip Street in a house with purple velvet curtains. Some people said he had been a diamond thief in his past. Some thought he was a porcupine trapper. Others said he was just a simple sausage maker. We simply don't know. And we'll have to live with that.

Richard Keiths was now in his seventies and his only way of getting about was on a mobility scooter, which his grandson Tommy had modified. It had go-faster flames and extra power cylinders and a super big fuel tank. Now Richard Keiths could reach eighteen miles per hour on Pegasus (which is what he called his scooter). There was just no way that old age was going to slow Mr Keiths down.

"Look out!" shouted Imelda, diving into a privet hedge as Mr Keiths motored towards them.

"Hairy hot chips!" shrieked Bobby. "He's not going to stop, he's not going to stop, he's not going to. . ."

But then he did stop, slamming on the brakes just as Bobby thought he was going to be splatted into boy mince.

Bobby peeled his fingers away from his face, panting. Mr Keiths was resting his elbow on Pegasus's handles, all relaxed and casual, like he hadn't nearly mobility scootered a child to death at all. He was stroking his chin like it was soft and peachy, when in fact it was stubbly and grey.

"Richard Keiths is the name," he said. "Who might you be, son?"

"He's Bobby from number four," shouted Imelda, pulling herself out of the hedge and whizzing up the road.

"What are you kids up to? Making trouble?"

asked Mr Keiths.

"We're trying to solve a whiskery mystery," blurted Imelda. "All the cats are being kidnapped. I mean catnapped. I mean kittynicked. I mean STOLEN!" she panted.

"Whoa, little lady, slow down," said Mr Keiths. "Those are some wild things you're speaking."

"But ALL the cats have disappeared, including Bobby's cat Conkers and Coriolanus from the Rhubarbs' house," she puffed. "We just don't know how or why or who did it."

"Well now, who's going to do a mean old thing like that?" asked Mr Keiths, smiling vaguely.

"It wasn't you, was it, Mr Keiths?" blurted Imelda, who was a bit of blurter.

Richard Keiths looked like he'd had an ice cube dropped down his trousers.

"Be very careful," he said, pointing slowly at Imelda, then at Bobby. "Be careful who you go accusing. I ain't a cat nabber or nicker. Sure, I drive a super cool mobility scooter and yeah, I'm kind of an outlaw on the street, but that don't mean I would steal cats. Ain't got the time, didn't do the crime."

"We're just eliminating suspects, that's all," said Bobby.

Richard Keiths rubbed his gnarly chin with his gnarly hand, looking off into the distance. For ages. It was just getting boring when he pinged back to life, like he'd be poked by an invisible stick.

"How do I know you two didn't do it, then?" he asked, squinting like a sleepy snake. "Sure, you look like nice kids, but summer holidays are long and boring. Maybe you're dreaming up your own mysteries, just for fun."

Imelda's jaw dropped open. Bobby went cherry red. As if Bobby would kidnap his own cat? It was outrageous. It was ridiculous. It *really* hurt his feelings.

"But. . ." Bobby spluttered.

"But nothing, boy," said Mr Keiths, revving Pegasus. He pointed his finger one more time at the children.

"Stay out of trouble, bambinos!" he said. "Let's keep things sweet on the street. . ."

12

Digging For Clues (Literally!)

The children went home. The run-in with Mr Keiths had made Bobby feel wobbly. Mr Keiths had been mean to the children, but was he mean enough to steal cats? Possibly, thought Bobby.

To cheer himself up, Bobby watched his favourite episode of *Meerkats In Maidstone*. In it, the meerkats finally worked out how to unlock

the back door and
have a nice run
about in the garden.
Wonderful stuff.

After lunch,
Imelda popped
round again. Pop!
The two played

Trump Trumps, where you compete with smell
cards. Bobby won with a Dairy Farm on a Hot Day

card, which trumped
Imelda's Goat's Breath
card. Then they
noticed Bobby's dad
loading up his car

with bags of Bitter-Choc Humphreys and Purple Bingo Flips and went out to help.

"What's up with you two?" asked Bobby's dad, noticing their long faces.

"We just can't work out where all the cats are going," Imelda blurted. "It's making our brains fizz!"

Bobby's dad didn't seem too bothered about the cats or the children's fizzing brains, either.

"Still on about the missing cats, eh?" he shrugged. "Why don't you get a nice hobby instead? Like gardening?"

"Gardening," said Bobby as PING! on went the light bulb of super-excellent brain waves

in Bobby's clever boy
brain. It was gardening
time! And not just
any old gardening.
Spy gardening.

The two knocked on
Mr Keiths' door.
He opened it,
leaning on a stick.

"We're here to
garden," said Imelda,
waving a dandelion
in the air.

"You said stay out of
trouble, Mr Keiths,

so we thought we could help out by doing some weeding," added Bobby. This wasn't strictly true. Because they were also there to have a nose around, searching for clues that Mr Keiths was the cat kidnapper of Pip Street. But they didn't tell Mr Keiths that.

Mr Keiths rubbed his chin, nodded and took them into the garden.

"You can weed everywhere, except here," he said, pointing his stick at a small flower bed with three big pebbles. On the pebbles were the names Benny, Kenny and Lenny.

"It's a memorial," he said, looking serious. "My cats. Loved every one of them. They were all taken too soon."

"What happened?" asked Imelda.

"It's hard to talk about," said Mr Keiths. But then he did talk about it.

"Benny was greedy. One day he broke into the fridge. Ate so much he exploded."

"Goodness," said Bobby, feeling sad, but also slightly wanting to laugh.

"Kenny fell

from a tree, landed

in my pants hanging

on the washing line, then

pinged off over the house

into the back of a passing truck. I couldn't get

outside fast enough to stop it. Who knows where

he is now."

"Doggy doughnuts of doom," said Imelda,

feeling sad, but also wanting to laugh, and then

noticing that Bobby wanted to laugh, which made

her want to laugh even more. You know how it gets. . .

"Lenny just flew away," said Mr Keiths, staring up at the clouds. "Literally."

The children were in real danger of erupting into giggles now, but Mr Keiths didn't notice. "My sixty-fifth birthday. Lenny got tied up in my helium balloons. Last time I saw him he was drifting towards the coast in a strong east wind."

The children were biting their lips and shaking now, big volcanoes of mirth bubbling up inside.

"We'll start over here," said Bobby, running with Imelda to the furthest part of the garden, where, behind a bush, they rolled about on the grass with their legs in the air, roaring with laughter.

When the giggle fit passed, Bobby said, "You know what this means, though, don't you, Imelda?"

"Richard Keiths is rubbish at looking after cats?" said Imelda.

"NO! Well, yes," said Bobby. "But what it *really* means is he's not guilty. He loves cats. It's obvious."

"Yes, yes, I see," said Imelda, nodding.

"So you know what *that* means?" added Bobby.

Imelda nodded. Then admitted that no, she didn't actually know what *that* means. . .

"It means," said Bobby, "there are only two suspects left on Pip Street."

"Nathan and your dad!" whispered Imelda, putting her hand over her mouth with shock.

"NO! Well, yes, but I really don't think it could be them," said Bobby. "No, I think the last two suspects must be Mother Pie and Jeff the Chalk. We need to investigate them more. I just need to work out how. . ."

13

He's Back! Back! Back!

It had been a busy day. Bobby's muscles had gone to soup and his brain had gone to smoothie, but that night he couldn't sleep. The mystery of the missing cats was proving so confusing. He still had two suspects to investigate and he was no closer to finding Conkers, which made his heart droop like a spaniel's ears.

He tossed and turned and eventually fell asleep,

dreaming that he and Conkers were riding on giant puffins, catching flying rainbows with nets made of mermaid hair. They were diving in and out of the clouds, laughing and laughing. Conkers was going *meow, meow* in his lovely deep cat voice, but it was muffled, what with the clouds and everything.

Meow, meow.

Hang on a minute, Conkers really was going meow, meow. Bobby woke with a start and flexed his ears. It was early morning.

"Meow, meow."

There it was again! Bobby would have known that meow anywhere.

"Conkers, Conkers, is that you?" shouted Bobby as he galloped downstairs like a champion racehorse who had been cooped up all day. He yanked open the front door. The meowing was coming from somewhere on Pip Street. But where?

"I'm coming, I'm coming," shouted Bobby, searching high, low and roughly in the middle, too.

"Conkers, meow one more time," he said, listening hard.

"Meow," came back the meow.

"There!" said Bobby, pointing at his dad's car. He raced over. And sure enough, there was Conkers, conked out underneath it.

"Oh, my pussy, my cat, my Conkers," said Bobby, scooping him into his arms with tears in his eyes. "Words fail me."

And there was silence.

But not for long. Imelda, just back from some early morning badger spotting, rushed over.

"It's Conkers!" said Bobby. "He's home. I *knew* he'd find his way back." **"Woo-hoo!"** shouted Imelda, jumping up and high-fiving a passing sparrow.

"Let's get him in," said Bobby, looking around nervously. He suddenly felt cold, as if a polar bear had opened a giant freezer to get a lolly out.

They gave Conkers a sachet of Captain Jason's Juicy Creations, and then Bobby took a good look at his long-lost cat and realized Conkers wasn't well. His tail was kinked and his paws were scraped. He looked like he'd been on a long journey, travelling far on his little pussy pins, with no tuna or currants to sustain him.

"I need to get you to the vet," said Bobby. "And fast."

14

Dr Mike, Vet Pet Detective

So Bobby took Conkers to the vet. But not just any old vet who treats guinea pigs with bad tummies. It was Dr Mike Browski, Vet Pet Detective. He spoke like an American cop in an American cop show, but really he was from Hemel Hempstead.

"Signs of bruising to the upper neck region," said Dr Mike, checking Conkers over.

"Like he was grabbed in a hurry. Two claws broken on his front right paw, three on his front left. Probably from trying to scratch his way out of a closed container. There is also evidence of rare plant life," he added, pulling some seeds out of Conkers' ear. "In-ter-esting," he said, staring at the seeds. "These come from the summer flowering Chinese pickle weed, which only grows in Rabid Pug Wood."

He looked up.

"I'd say your little friend here has been down to the woods, wouldn't you?" said Dr Mike. "But did he go on his own, or was he dragged down there, like

a terrified chipmunk in chains?"

15

A Surprising Discovery

Someone grabbed him – that's why he had the bruises on his neck – then shoved him into a box, then took him down to Rabid Pug Wood and dumped him there, thought Bobby as he walked out of Dr Mike's room – and straight into Jeff the Chalk!

Bobby was so shocked he almost dropped the cat basket. Jeff was so shocked he crashed into a shelf of Chappie Chops dog biscuits. The two stared at each other for a handful of seconds, and then Dr Mike appeared, looking for his next patient. He saw Bobby clutching his basket to his chest, and Jeff clutching a packet of Chappie Chops to his, and laughed.

"You guys OK?" he asked. "This is Jeffrey, my best vet nurse," he said to Bobby. "Animals love him and he loves animals."

Bobby smiled and then raced home, Conkers holding on to the basket with all his remaining claws as it swung madly. Bobby pelted round the corner of Pip Street and *WHAM!* collided with Imelda. Again!

"Oh bum crumble and cheese wees," shouted Imelda. "We must stop running into each other like this."

"Never mind, never mind," said Bobby, picking himself up. "I've got something to tell you. I've just seen Jeff the Chalk. At the vet's. He works there. Best nurse they have, said Dr Mike. Wouldn't hurt a gerbil. I don't think he did it."

Then Bobby explained how Conkers had been to Rabid Pug Wood.

"Perhaps we should go down there," said Bobby. "Maybe the other cats are there, too."

"No way," said Imelda, shaking her head.

"Not on my dead budgie's life. That place is far too dangerous!"

Bobby agreed. After what Nathan had told him about the wood, he didn't want to go down there any more than he wanted to clean toilets.

So instead, the children walked back to Bobby's house and looked at The List again. There was only one person left with a question mark next to her name. Mother Pie. Bobby looked nervously across the road. Was it her? Mother Pie? Could an old bid with bluish hair and a blinking habit *really* steal all the neighbourhood cats?

Bobby thought hard about what to do. He must not panic. There was no time for running about like your trousers were on fire shrieking "Alackadave!" Or for playing, either. Play is for children whose hearts are light and whose minds

think only of butterflies and magic strawberries,

but Bobby had a job to do. A mission to complete. A

whole bunch of cats to reunite with their families.

It was plan-making time.

16

A Plan Is Planned

Unfortunately, Bobby couldn't come up with anything, so he and Imelda went to the park to feed the ducks instead.

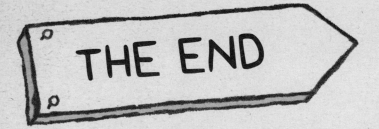

THE END

What?
Hang on,
no,
that's wrong.
Back to the
story.

16

VERSION 2
A Plan Is Planned
(No, Really, It Is This Time)

Have you ever made a plan? It takes planning.

But Bobby was an expert at plans and, after a big

dollop of thinking, he had it.

"I have it," he said.

The plan, code-named SHEILA, was

Bobby's biggest, fattest plan ever. It was a teensy

bit dangerous. It involved furry material from

the dressing-up box. It involved hours of sewing. It involved strong hearts and even stronger knees. It was inventive, it was creative; some

might say it was a little bit stupid. But forget about some. Don't listen to them. Some say a lot of things, most of which you can ignore.

Bobby and Imelda worked on S H E I L A all day. By evening, they were almost too tired to swallow or pull their pants up after a wee, even though they knew they had to.

"Sleep well, Imelda," said Bobby, before she went home. "Tomorrow is a big day."

"And I am a very small girl," said Imelda, winking.

17

He Thought He Saw
a Pussycat

Bobby woke early. Earlier than a baby with no

blackout blinds. But not as early as milkmen.

Let's say about six a.m.

As he dressed, Bobby's fingers trembled like

his hands were having an earthquake. Nerves!

He slipped out of the house and into Imelda's

back garden. She was peeping from her bedroom window, her two fluffy ears clearly visible.

Just a moment! Rewind! Two fluffy ears?

For yes, Imelda had two fluffy ears. And a tail. And whiskers. And a furry body. It was a disguise; a disguise to trump all disguises (in a beating-them way because it was so cool, not a guffing way). It was what the two had worked on so hard the day before. Imelda's tiny body was now squeezed into a cat suit. She had transformed from little girl to walloping big moggy. It was spectacular.

"Wow!" said Bobby, forgetting his nerves as Imelda appeared at the back door. "You look just like a cat!"

Imelda rubbed her cheeks against Bobby's leg and purred. She had all the catty moves. She was more cat-like than some cats. If she couldn't tempt the Pip Street kitty poacher, who could? Now the children would prove that cats were being stolen. The culprit would seize Imelda and Bobby would be there, recording it all with his camera – catching them in the act of nabbing a cat!

The children tiptoed on to the street and looked both ways. All was quiet.

Imelda gave a kitty thumbs up to Bobby and set off across the road.

"I'll be watching from the hedge," Bobby called.

"Be careful!"

18

Imelda In Danger

After about five minutes of pacing like a proper
pussycat, a door opened on the street and there
was . . . Mother Pie!

"Yes!" whispered Bobby.

Mother Pie stood on her doorstep wearing
beige slippers and a beige cardigan, looking
like the sweet old lady that she quite possibly
wasn't. Her face blinked hard, wrinkling up

like an old mushroom squashed in some lift doors.

"What's she going to do? What's she going to do?" muttered Bobby, straining to see through the hedgy greenness. She stared at Imelda, her face bouncing and rippling with blinks. Then suddenly she moved – fast – speed shuffling over to the giant kitty. Bobby stared, his heart pounding, his eyes as wide as plates.

Mother Pie stood over the big Imelda cat. Slowly, slowly, she leaned towards her.

Mother Pie's bony fingers were stretching out towards the furry body, and just as she was about to grab her . . . the rubbish lorry rumbled down the street and completely blocked Bobby's view!
No!

"Oh please move! Come on, come on," said Bobby, leaning this way and that to see what was going on.

Finally, it rumbled off and there, in front of Bobby, was ... NOTHING!

He sprang up, dropping his camera. Where was Imelda? Where was Mother Pie? What was going on? The plan code-named SHEILA didn't have a "what to do if everybody disappears in the time it takes a rubbish lorry to go past" bit. Bobby was at a total loss.

How long he stood on this spot, waiting for Imelda, I cannot say. His heart was racing, but his feet were not.

Finally, Mother Pie appeared on her doorstep.

She had beige shoes on now, but instead of a shopping trolley, she was pulling a wheelie bin.

"A very big bin for a very big cat," she chanted, as she wheeled it on to the pavement. "A very big bin for a very big cat! And that is, that is, that is, that."

Bobby gulped. A horrible hot whooshing zoomed up from his socks. She hadn't put Imelda in there? Surely not? A cat, in a bin? Who would do such a thing?

Mother Pie wheeled her bin down the road. She was heading for the rubbish lorry. Bobby followed, crouching behind cars, his heart going *boombittyboom*.

She was getting away, moving surprisingly fast for someone so old-ladyish. (For that is what an evil plan will do for shuffling oldies with a passion for wrongdoing – it gives them a little boost.)

Mother Pie was close to the bin men now, who were fixing the Pip Street bins to the back of the lorry. Its big metal arm lifted them up and flipped them over. The rubbish tumbled out, and then a metal squasher squished the bin bags into tiny black splats. The lorry didn't care what went

inside it. Old tissues and teabags and out-of-date ham were all the same to this huge machine. Overgrown cats? Who are really little girls in disguise? Sure, why not, it seemed to grin, throw one in. . .

At least this was what Bobby was thinking, and it was getting in the way of making a plan. So was that awful revving sound coming from behind him. *Arrghh!* He needed to think, work out what to do, but he was running out of time. Suddenly, the revving turned to a screeching of tyres and Richard Keiths slammed to a stop beside him, leaving skid marks all over the pavement.

"You're lucky I didn't run you over, son," said Mr Keiths, looking cross. "Standing around on pavements when Pegasus is fired up ain't a good idea. Move aside, boy."

"But, Mr Keiths," said Bobby, pointing madly down the road, "there's a cat in that bin and it's about to be squished."

"You fooling with me, son? Because I don't like to be messed with. Mess with me and you are entering a *world of pain*. . ."

And he did the whole pointing his finger thing again.

"Really, Mr Keiths, it's true," said Bobby, feeling like he was going to explode, like a firework that's been thrown into a volcano. "*Please* listen to me! If we don't do something, the cat will die!"

Mr Keiths squinted down the street towards

the bin lorry for a dangerously long time, then

suddenly revved Pegasus.

"Jump on, kiddo," he said. "No cat is getting

mashed on my watch."

"Oh thank you, thank you," shouted Bobby,

leaping on to Pegasus. "Now let's go, Mr Keiths.

Go! Go!"

He clutched Richard

Keiths' seat as the

engine revved,

and then Pegasus whammed forward. The pair belted down the street faster than whippets. It was one of the most exciting moments of Bobby's life.

Up ahead, Mother Pie's giant bin was hooked on to the back of the lorry and – oh sweet muffins of horror! – the arms began to lift.

"We need to go faster, Mr Keiths. Faster!" shouted Bobby. "They're going to tip it in, but it isn't a cat in there, it's Imelda!"

"What?" cried Mr Keiths. And then he grinned. "Hold on, Bobby, things are going to get choppy! It's time for turbo."

Nobody on Pip Street knew that Pegasus had a turbo button, but Mr Keiths had had one fitted for emergencies just like this. He pressed the turbo button now and the mobility scooter leapt forward at tip-top speed, scattering bin men and bins and a family of rabbits left and right.

Just as Bobby thought they were going to slam straight into the lorry, Richard Keiths hit the brakes.

Bobby flew off from behind him,

did a forward roll on the road,

sprang to his feet

and punched the lorry's red

STOP button hard.

Instantly, the lorry shuddered to a halt. There was an eerie silence, then Bobby shouted, "Get the bin down, get it down now! There's a little girl dressed as a cat in there and she's my friend."

The bin was slowly lowered, Bobby yanked open the lid and out popped Imelda, smelling of Scotch eggs, but otherwise fine. Imelda jumped into Bobby's arms and they hugged.

"Imelda, you're alive! I thought you were going to be bin-lorried to blithers!" said Bobby.

"It was close, wasn't it?" said Imelda. "I got tied up in my tail, then the Scotch egg stink made my head go woolly and it was so dark in there. I was really confused, Bobby, but I knew you'd save me, I knew it."

All the commotion had brought the people of Pip Street outside, and they rushed over to join the hug.

"Imelda, you're alive," said Bobby's mum.

"Imelda, you're alive," said Mrs Rhubarb, bursting into tears.

"Imelda, you're alive," said Mr Keiths, pulling up on Pegasus.

"Imelda, you're alive," said Bobby's dad, offering her a sweet. (It was a Peppermint Partrum.)

"**IMELDA, YOU'RE ALIVE!**" wrote Jeff the Chalk, in letters several centimetres high.

There was an outbreak of hugging, and while it went on, Mother Pie spied her chance to escape. She began to shuffle up the pavement, as fast as

her hip replacement would carry her.

"Wait, wait," shrieked Bobby, noticing her go. "It was Mother Pie who put Imelda in the bin. *And* she's the one who's been stealing all the cats."

The hugging stopped suddenly. Everyone looked at Mother Pie.

"I'm sure I don't know what the child is talking about," said Mother Pie, blinking a trio of energetic blinks. "Good day to you all, good day."

But as she continued to shuffle away, she was stopped by Nathan, marching down the street towards the crowd.

"No you don't," he said.

Mother Pie stood frozen to the spot.

"She left her front door open," shouted Nathan. "I went to close it and noticed this sitting in the hallway."

He wheeled the tartan shopping trolley with the padlock on it into the centre of the crowd.

"It's *covered* in cat hair!" said Nathan.

Mother Pie blinked hard and everyone jumped.

Up close, those blinks really gave you a shock.

"I hate them, I hate them, I do," she cried.

"Hate who?" said
everyone, looking
confused.

"Cats. Cats.
Wretched, stupid,
pointless cats!"
And she stamped her
old lady foot with the

last of her strength and sent a family of

ants to ant heaven on the Ant Afterlife Express.

"My childhood was ruined by cats," said Mother

Pie. "My mother loved cats more than me. They

were all over our house. . .!"

She shuddered at the memories.

"I vowed never to let one in my home, but one day, a cat sneaked into my living room ... and ... and ... AND DID A WHOOPSIE ON MY FAVOURITE RUG!"

Then Mother Pie blinked so hard her face looked like it was bungee jumping.

"*They* guessed the cats were being taken," she said, jabbing an old lady finger at the children.

"*They* knew I took that Conkers to the woods. They kept sticking their noses in where their noses weren't wanted. And I did put that giant cat in the bin – how could I know it was the girl?"

Mother Pie's black eyes stared meanly at

everyone. Nobody spoke. Then she turned to Jeff the Chalk.

"I thought you'd be pleased, Jeff," she said. "You hate the whoopsies as much as I do."

"I ONLY WANT A CLEAN STREET, NOT ONE WITH-OUT PETS" he wrote. "STEALING CATS IS NOT THE WAY. WE MUST LIVE TOGETHER PEACEFULLY."

It was a beautiful message and everyone looked off into the clouds, smiling at imaginary angels of peace floating on candyfloss.

"Bobby, I owe you an apology," said Bobby's dad. "I should have listened to you, instead of always rushing about with sweets on the brain."

Bobby nodded, great big sausages of relief rolling over him.

They hugged, and a giant roar filled the air. It wasn't bears; it was the people of Pip Street. Smiling, cheering, dancing and tossing sweeties into the sky. And while it rained Minty Twonks and Caramel Napalms and Silly Fruits and the people of Pip Street laughed and cheered, the police arrived and took Mother Pie off for some questions.

would you like a cup of tea? As the police car drove away, her lips were moving. What was she saying, this completely cat-hating old lady? What could it be?

"Nobody does, nobody does, nobody does a whoopsie on *my rug*!"

19

Peace and Pussycats
Return to Pip Street

That would be a lovely place to end the story, except let's not forget about the other cats. Tibbles and Kibbles and Felix and Shmelix and Pockets and Patches and Brian and Leslie and Bartholomew Garlic Bread Kittenpuss the Third.

A rescue party rushed to Rabid Pug Wood, where Mother Pie had dumped them, after wheeling them down there in her maximum security tartan shopping trolley. The cats were found, wandering about in a dark corner, confused and covered in seeds.

Brian was licking a squirrel called Graeme's tail. Patches thought he was a weasel. And there was Coriolanus, stuck up a tree, shivering under an oak leaf. It was a sad sight. But once the cats had come home and had an extra big serving of **FISH LUMPS**, they were perky as fireworks again.

So life settled down on Pip Street. The dogs went back to chasing the cats, which the cats didn't mind. It was fine, really, compared to what they had just been through. Bobby started going out with Jeff the Chalk on his chalking missions, and slowly, people began to clear up after their dogs. Nathan kept his brown dressing gown on all summer and Mr Keiths carried on driving around at seventeen or eighteen miles per hour.

"Turbo is only for emergencies," he would say, winking.

The week after Mother Pie was found out and all the cats came home, it was Bobby's birthday. His parents took him to **Pete's Pancake Pit Stop** for breakfast. Bobby had a Pete's Perfect

Pancake Leaning Tower of Plenty and as he ate happily, his dad announced that he had left the sweet-selling business and taken a job running the local crumpet factory.

"Does that mean we're staying on Pip Street?" asked Bobby.

Bobby's dad nodded.

"Woo-hoo!" shouted Bobby. "I think I'm going to like living on Pip Street. I think I'm going to like it a lot."

It was such good news that Bobby thought things couldn't get any better, but they did! He got home to find a package waiting for him on the doormat. It was his birthday present from Great Auntie Mo, all the way from Scotland. This was the present he always looked forward to most. It was sure to be something barmy and crazy. Something daft and maybe even dangerous.

Bobby ripped open the padded envelope and reached inside. His fingers touched a soft thing. Slowly, slowly, slowly he pulled out the soft thing and when he finally saw his gift, the gift he was so excited about, the gift that was sure to make him smile, Bobby said just one thing.

"Oh."

It was a pair of socks. A nice, sensible pair of socks. A nice, sensible pair of brown socks, in fact.

Sorry.

TURN OVER
FOR MORE

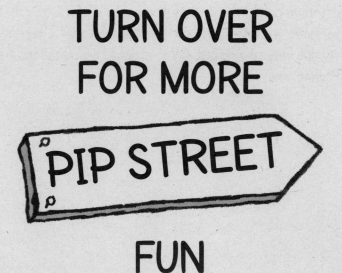

FUN

Quiz Time!

So you've got to the end of the book. Well done you.
But have you been paying attention? Really? There's
only one way to find out. With a quiz! Five questions,
starting now. . .

Question 1
Which of these TV shows does Bobby love?
A) Around Somerset on a trike with Lou Monty B) Meer-kats in Maidstone C) Spanners Through The Ages.

Question 2
Is Imelda Small
A) As tall as a giraffe b) About average height
c) Really quite tiny? (The clue is in the name...)

Question 3
What does Mother Pie smell of?
A) Marshmallows B) Salami C) Old lady talc mixed
with toffees and hair spray.

Question 4
Where are all the missing cats discovered?
A) In Buckingham Palace? B) Down the local Co-Op
C) Rabid Pug Wood.

Question 5
What helps Mr Keiths' mobility scooter Pegasus go extra
fast? A) Custard in the fuel tank B) Magic pixies C) Its
turbo button.

A Day in the Life of Conkers the Cat

Conkers is cool, and when he's not being catnicked or having to escape from spooky woodlands, he knows how to have a good time. Check out his typical schedule. . .

8am. Get up. Lick paws. Breakfast. Visit garden for fresh air and a little wee-wee. Wave Bobby off to school. Go back to sleep.

12pm. Get up. Lick paws. Scratch carpet. Go back to sleep.

3pm. Get up. Visit garden for fresh air etc. Position self in prime stroking spot on garden wall for Bobby's return from school. Get stroked. Go back to sleep.

7pm. Get up. Try to lick humans' dinner plates. Practise karate on passing moth. Go back to sleep.

8.30pm. Run up and down upstairs corridor for one minute precisely while Bobby brushes his teeth. Visit garden for fresh air and a little poo-poo. Bedtime.

And that's how Conkers rolls.

See if you can find all the cats on Pip Street

(Hint: there are 10 cats hiding)

A whiskery wordsearch

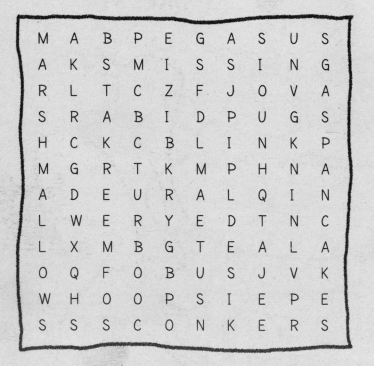

```
M A B P E G A S U S
A K S M I S S I N G
R L T C Z F J O V A
S R A B I D P U G S
H C K C B L I N K P
M G R T K M P H N A
A D E U R A L Q I N
L W E R Y E D T N C
L X M B G T E A L A
O Q F O B U S J V K
W H O O P S I E P E
S S S C O N K E R S
```

Have a look for these hidden words:

Marshmallows	Meerkats	Pancakes
Conkers	Pip	Turbo
Rabid Pug	Whoopsie	Missing
Pegasus	Alackadave	Blink

Can you help Bobby find Conkers?

Pip Street is having its very own crumpet

bake-off and everyone is taking part.

Harmless fun?

Not exactly...

The competition is doomed unless brave

Bobby Cobbler can outsmart his nasty neighbour

Pompey Pasty, who is determined to

win by any means...

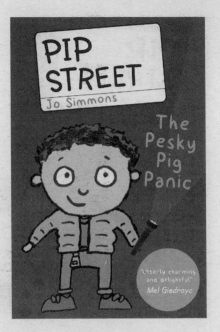

Torches at the ready!

The lights are out on Pip Street.

But what's causing the bothersome blackouts?

And does a mysterious pig have

anything to do with them?

Bobby Cobbler is on the case — or he will be,

once he gets over his greatest fear: the dark!

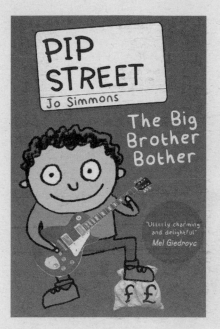

Who is this mysterious stranger, racing onto

Pip Street in a sleigh pulled by dogs?

It's Richard Keiths' bad-news brother,

Walter, with a head full of naughty

plans and horrible threats.

Can Bobby boot out this bothersome brother

and save the street from peril?